For my family.
For Andrew.

BOX OF TRICKS
A JONATHAN CAPE BOOK 978 0 224 08344 7
Published in Great Britain by Jonathan Cape,
an imprint of Random House Children's Books
A Random House Group Company

This edition published 2009
1 3 5 7 9 10 8 6 4 2

RANDOM HOUSE CHILDREN'S BOOKS
61–63 Uxbridge Road, London W5 5SA

www.kidsatrandomhouse.co.uk
www.rbooks.co.uk

Addresses for companies within The Random House Group Limited can be found at
www.randomhouse.co.uk/offices.htm

THE RANDOM HOUSE GROUP Limited Reg. No. 954009
A CIP catalogue record for this book is available from the British Library.

Printed in Singapore

handle with care
contains magic

Box of Tricks

A magical story
by Katie Cleminson

Jonathan Cape
London

On her birthday,
Eva was given a
very special present.

She opened it,
jumped in . . .

. . . and became a master magician.

TA-DAH!

For her first trick, she wished for what she most wanted in the whole world: a pet called Monty.

Monty turned out to be rather large.

For her next trick,

Eva pulled rabbits out of hats.

Then, with a flick of her wand

she made things float in the air.

For her biggest trick of all, Eva threw a huge party.

There was lots of

delicious food,

the very best musicians . . .

and
plenty
of
dancing.

When everyone had danced their socks off,

Eva
shut her eyes,
clicked her
fingers . . .

and everything vanished . . .

Well,
not quite
everything.